Lulu and the Artist

English edition copyright © 1992 by The Child's World, Inc.
French edition © 1988 by Casterman
All rights reserved. No part of this book may be
reproduced or utilized in any form or by any means
without written permission from the Publisher.
Printed in the United States of America.

Distributed to Schools and libraries
in the United States by
ENCYCLOPAEDIA BRITANNICA EDUCATIONAL CORP
310 South Michigan Ave.
Chicago, Illinois 60604

ISBN 089565-741-4
Library of Congress Cataloging-in-Publication Data
available upon request

Lulu and

the Artist

A Lulu and Banana Story

author: Lionel Koechlin
illustrator: Annette Tamarkin Hatwell

The Child's World
Mankato, Minnesota

Every morning Lulu gets dressed
as fast as she can.
Then she searches the apartment.

She explores the cellar and the attic. She pokes her nose into the dresser drawers and peeks behind the curtains.

Every morning Banana asks her,

"Whatever are you looking for, Lulu?"

"I'm looking for my dog."

"You've never had a dog, Lulu dear, and it's just as well, because dogs often have bad manners. Please drink your cocoa!"

But in Lulu's memory there's a dog that comes by at night, carrying a box of paints, and who laughs as he tells her, "I'll paint your portrait soon!"

Before setting off for school today, Lulu empties her piggy bank.

On the way she buys a bag of caramels at the grocery store, and sits down on a bench to write a message on a sheet of paper. Lulu sticks the message on the back of the policeman who helps pedestrians across the road.

School is over now. The policeman and the children are going home. While they are having a snack in front of the television, Lulu is impatiently waiting for her dog.

Arsenio is the first person to arrive with a dog. Lulu
hesitates, then says, "That's not my dog; my dog
cleans his teeth. But have a caramel anyway."

Arthur is next. He's in disguise. Lulu thinks a
moment, then says, "My dog is not a reindeer. But
have a caramel anyway."

Alphonse comes along with the third dog. Lulu sighs:
"My dog is not shy. But have a caramel anyway."

Alice introduces her dog next. Lulu says: "My dog
did not come out of an egg. But have a caramel
anyway."

Andy has a dog for Lulu, too. "Come now! My dog
doesn't live in the desert! But have a caramel
anyway."

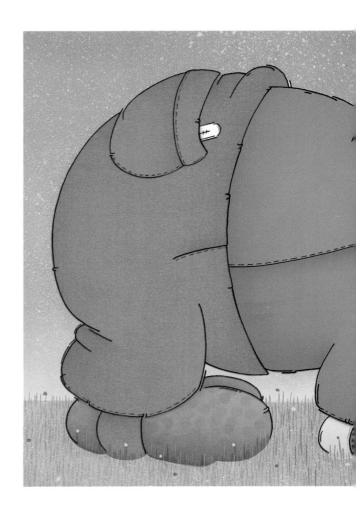

Annie has read the message, too. "My dog doesn't
have anything wrong with him," says Lulu, "He
hasn't been bitten by any mosquitoes. But have a
caramel anyway."

It's very late and the caramel bag is empty.
Banana arrives. He is cross.

"I've been looking for you everywhere, Lulu, I've
been very worried and the soup is cold now. Let's go
home!"

But Lulu still wants to wait a bit longer. So Banana
sits down, grumbling, and puts Lulu on his lap.

Time passes.

At midnight, a dog arrives at last. He is all alone.

Lulu says, "I know who you are."

"Don't move," answers the artist, "I'm going to paint your portrait."

Banana interrupts him,

"Come home with us, it'll be nice to have a plateful of reheated soup to eat. And when you've finished Lulu's portrait, you can do mine."

"I'll never be able to draw a cat; it's much too difficult," replies the artist.

"Oh," answers Banana, "We have the whole night ahead of us."

THE CHILD'S WORLD LIBRARY

A DAY AT HOME

A PAL FOR MARTIN

APARTMENT FOR RENT

CHARLOTTE AND LEO

THE CHILLY BEAR

THE CRYING CAT

THE HEN WITH THE WOODEN LEG

IF SOPHIE

JOURNEY IN A SHELL

KRUSTNKRUM!

THE LAZY BEAVER

LEONA DEVOURS BOOKS

THE LOVE AFFAIR OF MR. DING AND MRS. DONG

LULU AND THE ARTIST

THE MAGIC SHOES

THE NEXT BALCONY DOWN

OLD MR. BENNET'S CARROTS

THE RANGER SMOKES TOO MUCH

RIVER AT RISK

SCATTERBRAIN SAM

THE TALE OF THE KITE

TIM TIDIES UP

TOMORROW WILL BE A NICE DAY

THE TREE POACHERS